Eight Nights
to win her
Heart

RONI DENHOLTZ

Acknowledgements : Many thanks to my wonderful editor, formatter, and cover designer Judi Fennell!

Eight nights had never been more important…

"Please give me a chance," Ben rushed on.

Roslyn's chest tightened.

"*Please.*" This time his voice dropped low. "Hanukkah starts Sunday. It's the holiday of miracles. Please let me see you every night of Hanukkah."

"Hanukkah? Why—"

"Give me those eight nights. If I can't convince you I love you, that I deserve another chance—if you're not convinced that my love will last more than eight days, then I'll go away quietly, and leave you alone. For good."

She hesitated, her heart seeming to splinter. Should she give him another chance? Would it hurt either of them?

Would eight days and nights make a difference in the grand scheme of things? It was only eight days. Eight nights.

Hanukkah, the holiday of miracles…

"Please give me eight nights to win your heart," he whispered.

DEDICATION

To two very special friends,
Judie and Don Fast
Thank you for your friendship and all your support!

PROLOGUE

"So what's the emergency, bro?"

Ben Jaffe turned to find his closest friend, Dave, whom he'd called only fifteen minutes ago, standing right behind him as he sat at the bar.

Ben sighed, toying with his glass of vodka. His second, already.

"She broke up with me," he said, his voice cracking.

"Roslyn broke up with you? You've got to be kidding." Dave slid onto the empty barstool beside Ben. "I thought she was crazy about you!"

"She says she is." Ben stared at the clear drink, chunks of ice reflecting the low bar lights. From behind him loud laughter came from a group at a nearby table.

"Huh?" Dave frowned. "Tell me from the beginning. Didn't you say yesterday she invited you over for tonight?"

On a Tuesday, the Jersey City bar two blocks from Ben's apartment wasn't too crowded. Several TVs showed a basketball game in progress, the New York Knicks playing a team from out west. For once he didn't give a damn.

"Thanks for coming," Ben said. Dave lived only four blocks from Ben, but had agreed to meet him the minute he heard Ben's distressed voice. "I—" he couldn't help feeling like crap. He lifted the glass and took another swallow.

"You know I'm here for you. A Miller," he said to the bartender who stood in front of them. "So—tell me what happened?"

"I got there right on time, seven thirty," Ben said. "Roslyn looked gorgeous, even in a sweater and jeans. I tried to kiss her, but she pushed me away and said she wanted to talk."

"Uh oh. When a woman says that, it's generally not good."

"Yeah. Anyway, we sat down, and she said we've been going out now for four years. When she said that, I immediately got nervous."

"Sounds like she was going to give you The Ultimatum," Dave said. He lifted his beer.

"That's what I was afraid of. But she didn't. She said she thought we should break up. Move on."

"The Ultimatum in disguise," Dave said. taking a swig.

"No. She said she would never do that. See, her cousin Brad went with Ruth Ann for three years, and Ruth Ann gave him an ultimatum; either they get married, or she'd drop him. So—they got married."

"And?" Dave asked, raising his eyebrows.

Again, laughter burst from the group behind them. It only made Ben feel more isolated.

"They got married a few years ago—and Brad is miserable. Totally miserable."

"Poor guy."

"So, Roslyn decided she would never put anyone through that. She'd never put *me* through that." He saw her in his mind's eye, so serious, sitting on the couch facing him. Her beautiful dark hair waving over her shoulders. Tears in her eyes as she spoke.

"'I love you too much to try to force you to marry me' she said," Ben quoted her exact words. "I'd rather break it off and remain friends than coerce you into something you don't want."

"What was your response?" Dave asked.

"Of course I reminded her that I'd always said someday we'd get married," Ben quickly answered his friend. "And—we will. When I'm ready.

"But she snapped back that I'd never be ready," he continued. "She knew how I was afraid of commitment, what with my parent's horrible divorce and all the arguments they had before—and after. And she said she would never want to marry someone who *didn't* totally want that commitment with her. Then she told me a story I hadn't heard before. Her aunt Ann went with this guy for ten years, planning to marry him. After that time he suddenly threw her over and married someone else. She says she doesn't want that to happen to her."

"Ahhh… " Dave drew out the syllable. "So, the two of you broke up"

"Not exactly. I asked her to give me a little more time. She refused, and said four years was enough. I can't even—blame her." His voice cracked. His insides tightened as he recalled her words. "I—I don't want to lose her. I do love her, Dave. It's just that I've been afraid. But even last week, I was thinking we should take our relationship to the next level--get engaged."

"Did you tell her that?"

He nodded. "Yes, but I don't think she believed me. She practically pushed me out the door. So, I left.

And came here, and called you." He took a gulp of his drink this time, the alcohol burning a path down his throat.

"So that's it?"

"No! I don't want to lose her. I have to think of some way to win her back.. I love her. I do want to end up with her." As he said the words, he knew how true they were. Despite all the times he'd declared he wasn't sure if he'd ever marry, and then the times he said he'd marry *later*, he did want Roslyn in his life. Permanently. She was beautiful, she was kind and sweet, and fun. The two of them were a team.

"I love her," he declared. "She's really the best thing that ever happened to me. I don't want—" he choked—"to lose her." He shut his eyes for a moment, picturing Roslyn. She'd was petite, with dark, silky hair and wide brown eyes. She was usually smiling.

But not tonight.

"What are you going to do?" Dave's words caused Ben's eyes to snap open. He observed his friend drinking more beer.

"I don't know! I have to win her back—" he stared miserably at his drink, shaking it slightly, the ice clinking against the glass with a musical sound.

"Why don't you call her and try to talk some more?"

"If I had some way to convince her—" Ben began. Raising his eyes, he caught sight of another TV in the corner. This one was tuned to a local news station, and a reporter was discussing Hanukkah, a large menorah by his side, and the celebrations of the holiday in a town near here.

"They'll be hosting a giant Menorah lighting," the reporter said enthusiastically.

Hanukkah. The holiday of miracles, when the oil in the temple lasted eight days and nights instead of the expected one. The holiday was only five days away.

An idea began to burn inside of him. Like the candles they would light on the menorah.

"I can use Hanukkah," Ben whispered.

"What?" Dave stared at him.

"I can use the eight days of Hanukkah to try to persuade her to give me another chance. That gives me eight nights to change her mind."

"Well, Hanukkah *is* the holiday of miracles," Dave stated.

Eight nights to win her over, Ben thought.

Eight nights.

***

Roslyn Stein had shed enough tears lately to create a stream. A river. She'd never cried so much.

Or had her stomach in knots like this for weeks, agonizing with her decision to break it off with the only man she'd ever truly loved.

But she couldn't keep going on like this. She just *couldn't.*

She wanted white lace and wedding vows. She wanted a partner through the highs and lows of life. She wanted children—children who had two caring parents and a complete family unit. She didn't want to be a single mom, struggling without a partner; or to have kids who always wondered why they had no father. She wanted it *all*.

But she'd slowly faced the fact that she'd never have that with Ben. His parent's acrimonious divorce had left him skeptical and untrusting of the institution of marriage. She got that, she truly did. As a social worker she'd seen how terrible marriages could affect family members.

She'd never try to coerce Ben into something he didn't want. She loved him too much to try to force him into marriage.

And she respected herself too much to go on like this, wishing and hoping for something she'd realized was not going to happen.

Oh, she'd considered trying to force the issue. But seeing how unhappy her cousin Brad was—Brad, whose wife had told him marry her or else she was done—she'd never want to do that to a man. Especially Ben, who had so many wonderful qualities. Empathy and caring, humor, intelligence, compassion for children and animals—all she wanted in a man.

And she certainly didn't want to end up like her Aunt Ann. She's heard the stories many times—Ann had dated a man—a doctor Roslyn's grandmother would say in a horrified voice—"how could a doctor to that?" Ann had hung on for ten years, waiting for him to pop the question. Everyone said she'd given up the best years of her life, waiting for him through college, medical school, his internship, residency—establishing himself as a physician. And when he finally had completed those things and she was sure he was going to propose and they'd live happily ever after—he'd turned around, told Ann he'd fallen in love with a nurse at the hospital, and was dropping her. Like a hot potato.

And within a year he'd married that nurse and forgotten all about his devoted girlfriend.

Roslyn had had a spirited argument with her grandmother, Tema, who said she, Tema, had cried buckets because "Ann couldn't keep hold of a doctor." Roslyn had been amazed, then angry, that her grandmother considered it a loss because that *schmuck* was a doctor. "He treated Ann so badly!" she'd declared to her grandmother many times.

"If Ann had had a firm grip on him, it would never have happened," her Grandmother had moaned. "Then she had no one!" Apparently, losing a doctor almost-fiancé was a fate worse than death in her grandmother's crazy view.

Her aunt had married hastily a few years later—someone who was not a doctor, on the rebound, family members had whispered. Just so she could get married, they'd said. And she had never seemed happy when Roslyn saw her. Now, her aunt was gone. She'd neglected her health, ate and drank too much, and complications from diabetes plus heart problems had caused an early death.

Roslyn didn't want that. She loved Ben too much to push the idea of marriage. Who wanted a husband who didn't want her? A man who loved her, as he'd said often enough, but not enough for a life time commitment?

It was while watching the popular show about women choosing bridal gowns that she'd realized the truth.

She wanted to get married. And if Ben didn't want that… there was no reason to stretch this out for ten years like her aunt had. So, she'd broken it off with Ben last night.

It was Wednesday morning now, and she hadn't slept well. Even though she'd decided to take the day off and go shopping with her best friend Amanda—Roslyn needed Hanukkah gifts for her brother and sister, and Christmas gifts for a few friends and co-workers—she'd woken at her usual time, 7 o'clock. Thoughts had come rushing back about the scene with Ben the night before, and, unable to sleep, she'd stumbled into the kitchen to make coffee.

She watched the weather channel while she had her breakfast and two cups of coffee, then got dressed. Amanda would be picking her up at 9 so they could get an early start.

About fifteen minutes before Amanda was going to pick her up, her cellphone buzzed. It was probably Amanda, running late as usual, Roslyn assumed. She grabbed the phone. "Hi Amanda," she said, without even looking at the face of the phone.

"Roslyn? It's Ben."

His deep, masculine voice sent a shock wave through her system. She hadn't expected him to call or try to get in touch with her in any way.

"Ben?" she croaked.

"I miss you," he began. "I want to see you again. I *need* to see you."

"I don't think that's a good idea," she said. She wanted to sound firm, but her voice came out shaky.

"*Please.* I'm lost without you. You know I love you."

"Look, Ben, you know I'd never try to coerce—" she gripped the chair she was standing near. Her palm pressed against the smooth texture of the cloth back.

"I know. You're not," he interrupted. "Please give me a chance to make this right. I did a lot of thinking last night. I love you."

"I love you too, but that's not the point—"

"Please give me a chance," he rushed on.

Her chest tightened.

"*Please.*" This time his voice dropped low. "Hanukkah starts Sunday. It's the holiday of miracles. Please let me see you every night of Hanukkah."

"Hanukkah? Why—"

"Give me those eight nights. If I can't convince you I love you, that I deserve another chance—if you're not convinced that my love will last more than eight days, then I'll go away quietly, and leave you alone. For good."

She hesitated, her heart seeming to splinter. Should she give him another chance? Would it hurt either of them?

Would eight days and nights make a difference in the grand scheme of things? It was only eight days. Eight nights.

Hanukkah, the holiday of miracles…

"Please give me eight nights to win your heart," he whispered.

She sighed. "Alright." *I hope I don't regret this.*

Yet, her heart felt lighter and happier at the thought of seeing him at least eight more times.

CHAPTER I

First Night of Hanukkah

She didn't think she'd been this nervous about seeing Ben, ever. Not even on their first date.

She'd wanted to impress him that night He'd invited her to go out for dinner, and she had suggested her favorite Italian place, which was nearby.

They'd met at her cousin Jacob's Bar Mitzvah. Jacob was one of her youngest cousins. Ben's father and Roslyn's uncle were partners in their law firm, so Ben's whole family had been invited. His "new" family. His father and his new wife; Ben and his brother; and his step sister and brother.

Ben had taken her uncle aside and asked him who "that gorgeous girl" was, she learned later. Uncle Mitch had introduced them, and the rest was history.

Ben was not only handsome, but confident, polished, and intelligent. She'd been a little nervous about their first date.

But this evening, noticing how her hands shook, she knew she was much more nervous.

When she'd gone shopping with Amanda, her friend had urged her to give Ben that chance. "Otherwise, you'll always wonder if maybe it would have worked," Amanda had declared.

Now Roslyn wondered if a clean break would have been better.

She stared at the brass menorah she'd put on her entry way table. It had belonged to her grandmother, and now it was hers. Her windowsills were too narrow to put anything on, so this would have to do. She'd already put the first candle and the Shamash in the menorah, both candles a light blue, and the box of matches lay beside the menorah. Ben had texted he'd like to light the menorah together.

"But you know I won't leave candles burning when we go out," she'd protested. "I won't even leave them in the sink like my grandmother used to do." They were supposed to leave the candles lit until they burned out; but knowing that could be hazardous, she's always blown them out if she had to leave her home.

"Agreed," he'd said. "Maybe we can light them together another night."

She'd murmured "okay" at his words. She lit the Shamash, then touched the flame to the first candle as she recited the prayer. Returning the Shamash to its holder, she stared at the steady, small flames. She wondered if Ben would try to convince her to go to bed with him. They'd always burned up the sheets together. When she'd first considered breaking up with Ben, she'd realized she would miss not only the great sex, but the sense of closeness they always shared afterwards. She doubted she'd find that with someone else. Decorating for the holidays had always been a pleasure, but this year she'd had mixed feelings about it, knowing it could be her last Hanukkah with Ben.

The doorbell rang, interrupting her depressing thought.

"Coming," she called, smoothing her hands over her black pants. She moved to the door as heart beat increased.

This is ridiculous. It's just Ben.

She took a deep breath and opened the door.

Ben stood there, looking as handsome as always. He wore a charcoal gray coat which was open, revealing a dark blue sweater, a black shirt collar peeking out from underneath the V-neck. Dark blue jeans and casual loafers completed the picture. He looked like a professional who was dressed to go out on a cold winter evening. Which was exactly what he was.

His broad shoulders, handsome face, and masculine features were so evident that she felt the familiar flutters she always got after not seeing him for a few days. Which did happen sometimes, with their busy work schedules.

But tonight, she caught something different in his expression. Almost a look of desperation.

She swallowed. "Hi."

"Hi," he said with a smile, and that look disappeared.

He glanced at the menorah on the table in the entryway, and disappointment crossed his face. "I see you lit the candles. I was hoping you'd wait for me."

Lighting them together in the past had been a shared intimacy which she'd always enjoyed. "Well, it was dark; and I need to blow them out when we leave," she explained. "So, I went ahead." She wasn't sure she wanted to light them with him right now, anyway.

She noticed he held a wrapped package in his hand. It had blue and white Hanukkah motifs on the wrapping paper and a big blue bow.

"Wait for me to light them with you tomorrow?" he asked.

She hesitated. Did she want to do that with him? Seeing his eager expression, she relented. "Alright." She wanted to kick herself for sounding so breathless. Like his very nearness shook her.

Truthfully, it did.

He held out the package to her. "Happy Hanukkah."

"Come in and sit down." She led the way to her brown sectional couch, and they sank down on the seats.

The package wasn't large, and she tore the paper open in her usual, messy fashion. She'd always been too anxious to reveal a present to do it neatly.

The simple gold square box had the insignia of a jewelry store chain on it.

He wouldn't—he couldn't—she swallowed. It wasn't the shape of an engagement ring. At this point in their relationship, that would be way too presumptuous, after their break-up.

She opened the box, her heart beating hard. Inside were two silver earrings, silver dreidels hanging on small hoops.

"Ohhh!" she breathed. "These are lovely!"

"I don't think you have anything like this," he said, scooting a little closer.

"No. These are great!" She stood and walked over to the mirror in the entryway above the table. Her face glowed in the candlelight as she fumbled to take off her gold hoop earrings, then to insert the new ones.

He followed her. He must have seen her hands trembling, because he said "here," in a low, masculine rumble. He took the first earring from her and inserted it in her ear, adding the backing. As he did his fingers brushed the skin behind her ear.

She shivered from the touch, and met his eyes in the mirror.

She saw raw desire in his expression, and her heartrate increased.

They'd always had great sexual chemistry, and whenever she saw *that* expression in his eyes, her body never failed to respond, tightening with yearning. Just as it did now.

She wanted to groan. She was giving him another chance—but she didn't want to simply jump into bed with Ben!

When he finished with the earrings, he bent down and gave her a soft kiss on the cheek. Tingles moved through her.

"I'm ready to go," she said, striving to make her voice even.

He grinned at her in the mirror, his eyes glowing, an almost feral expression on his face. She felt that familiar thrumming through her body. And the shot of excitement that always accompanied it.

*****

They went to their favorite Italian restaurant near the condo she rented, a condo that was not far from the medical rehabilitation center where she worked. Roslyn wondered if Ben had suggested eating there since they had so many good memories from this restaurant.

He ordered seafood fra diavolo. and beer, while she asked for chicken parmigiana and a white wine.

"How's work going?" he asked as the waitress brought their drinks over.

"Good." She sipped her wine. She was a social worker at the center, working with injured adults who needed physical therapy and nursing care, and helping them to get on-going care when they returned home. "This week I got two patients back who had been in earlier this year. They'd both injured themselves again."

"I know you get a lot of repeat patients," he observed.

"Yes." She sighed. "I try to get them to make changes in their lives so they're less likely to be injured—but they don't always listen. I always feel bad when they return with new injuries."

She reached for the crusty bread the waiter brought over, and as she did, he covered her hand with his.

"You always care about your patients," he said solemnly. "I don't know anyone who is as caring as you."

She withdrew her hand. "Thanks."

"I mean it," he continued. "You're such a caring person. I hope you know how much I appreciate that."

She raised her eyebrows. "Do you?"

"Absolutely." Again, he covered her hand with this. This time, he squeezed it.

She felt flustered. He sounded so sincere. Did he really think that? His eyes were earnest as they met hers.

She grabbed the bread and changed the topic. She didn't want to have this discussion. Not yet.

She asked about his job. He was a corporate lawyer, working near Wall Street. He hadn't wanted to work in the firm owned by his father and her uncle. But her sister had recently become a lawyer and gone to work there. He told her that his father had mentioned she was a hard worker.

They spoke as they ate the delicious food. As they were finishing, she couldn't suppress a yawn. She hadn't been sleeping well since their break-up.

"I know it's getting late," he said. "And tomorrow's Monday and we have to be at work."

"Yes. And I have meetings with three different families in the morning," she said.

He drove the short distance to her home and walked her to the door. After she unlocked it, she turned to say goodnight.

"I'll see you tomorrow," he said, and she caught that glimmer in his eyes again. "Is six o'clock good for dinner?'

"Six? Will you be able to get out of the city that soon?" Commuting from New York to Jersey City even by train often meant delays; and then he'd be driving here to Franklin, an hour away.

"I'll manage. I can leave work early," he stated.

She raised her brows. His job was so important to him, and he was often late because of it. "Really?" She'd always found it so annoying when he ran late.

"Really," he said emphatically. Bending forward, he gave her a chaste kiss on her forehead. "Goodnight, Roslyn."

Her forehead tingled from the short kiss. "Goodnight." She walked in, turned, and watched him walk to his car. Just before getting in, he waved.

She waved back, and shut the door, leaning against it.

He still had the power to make her heart beat faster.

And right now, she wasn't happy about that.

CHAPTER II

Second Night of Hanukkah

As he drove to Roslyn's place on Monday, Ben couldn't help picturing her as she'd looked yesterday. She'd dressed in nice pants and a sweater that hinted at her curves. Her satiny hair and kissable lips were enough to make any man salivate, and it had been hard not to pull her into his arms often last night.

Especially since, although she dressed in a classy, not slutty way, he knew the gorgeous body that those clothes covered up. And her penchant for wearing lacy, sexy lingerie.

But Roslyn was so much more than physically beautiful. She was compassionate, caring, and thoughtful. As she'd spoken about her patients, that fact had reverberated through him. The thought of living without her in his life made him freeze all over.

He *had to* win her back.

He'd brought brisket and potato pancakes from a deli near where he worked today before he took the train back to Jersey City. He wanted to prove he could be as considerate as she was. That he would be more thoughtful from now on.

He'd texted Roslyn and told her they'd have a

casual dinner together. Then, he was taking her to a Menorah lighting in a nearby town. He'd never been to a public menorah lighting--but it sounded like a fun thing to do. It was cold but not raining or windy tonight, so the weather should cooperate.

Last night, when he arrived back at his condo, he'd brainstormed the rest of the eight nights he was spending with her. He had plans for each one now, and couldn't wait until the eighth night.

On the last night, his gift would be a ring, and he'd ask her to be his wife. He fervently hoped she would accept.

Because the more time that passed, the more he wanted to marry her. Without Roslyn, without knowing she was there for him, he'd felt a huge hole in his life.

He turned off the highway now and onto the main road near her rented condo. It was a cute place, and he knew she hoped to buy it or one that was similar in the same development when she'd saved up a little more money.

He was lucky. His salary plus an inheritance from his grandfather had meant he was able to buy a beautiful, almost-new condo in Jersey City in a great location. He'd spent many happy hours on weekends there with Roslyn. Many of those hours in bed. She might think they had a problem with their relationship because he was reluctant to commit, but they'd never had a problem in bed. Their love-making had been absolutely fantastic.

He knew she was right about his commitment phobia—he'd been very reluctant to get married. And he knew exactly why.

When he was fourteen, his father had announced he was leaving his mother for another woman—a woman from their temple, a woman he'd been having an affair with for a year. She was a little younger, sexier, and later he'd observed much more aggressive than his own mother.

It had torn their family in two. His older brother and he had been devastated; his mother, heartbroken.

Meanwhile his soon-to-be step mom had taken over his father, body and soul, thrusting her kids into their fractured family, then declaring how wonderful it was that they could all "get along" although they couldn't. And didn't.

Oh, now that they were adults they got along alright. His step-sister lived in Old Bridge—not too far away—and actually had a decent relationship with him and his brother. His step-brother lived in the Washington DC area and had little to do with any of them, or his mother or Ben's father. The only one he seemed close to was his own father.

Ben's mother had had a string of boyfriends after the divorce—going from one man to another, trying to find love. Ben had hated the men she paraded in front of her kids. He'd long ago realized she was trying to make herself feel good and some of the men, while not terrible people, were not great either. Last spring she'd broken up with a guy she'd been with for two years, and right now was unattached. Which, he thought, was a good thing for her. Let her find out exactly what she wanted. Meanwhile, his step-siblings' father had married again— but not for a number of years after the divorce.

Ben made a few turns and now he pulled into the parking lot of Roslyn's condo development. Stepping out of the car, he walked rapidly to her unit and rang the doorbell.

In his hand, he held another gift. A necklace to match the dreidel earrings. He was following the tradition of a present for every night of Hanukkah. In his family, the children had always gotten gifts each night until they turned 13—adults in the eyes of Judaism. Most families he knew did that, and Roslyn's had also. Not that he thought of her as a child. It just seemed like a thoughtful, romantic thing to do.

He was glad he'd texted her and asked her to wait til he got there to light the candles. He thought it would be a warm way to share the holiday, lighting them together. When she opened the door, he caught sight of the menorah, ready and waiting with two candles plus the Shamash.

"Hi! Happy Hanukkah," he said, and stepped inside, handing the package to her. His hand brushed her soft one. He noticed immediately that she was wearing the dreidel earrings he'd given her last night.

"Another gift?" she asked lightly. "You're spoiling me, Ben. Only children get gifts every night."

"You deserve much more," he said solemnly. Because she did. She deserved pampering. A stab of guilt hit him. He'd been good to her, yes, in the past… but had he pampered her? A loving girlfriend should be spoiled, a little, he thought. And he determined he wouldn't forget that idea.

She blushed. "Thanks." As he shrugged out of his coat, she tore open the paper, and gasped. "Oh, this matches the earrings!" She lifted the silver necklace. "Thank you!"

She fumbled with the necklace, trying to catch the clasp in the back.

"Allow me." He moved towards her. Lifting her

silky, dark hair, he easily put the necklace on, tugging slightly at the clasp to be sure it was secure.

And while he bent forward, he breathed in the sexy fragrance she wore. Not the plain floral fragrance she usually wore during the week, but the one she saved for weekends when she was around him—because she knew he liked it.

He leaned closer, breathing in the perfume and the scent that was Roslyn, uniquely her, feminine and appealing.

He heard her catch her breath and then she quickly moved away. Turning, she looked in the mirror. "This is perfect." She smiled, but he saw hesitancy in her expression.

Shit. Had he come on too strong, gotten too close? The last thing he wanted was to make her uneasy around him.

But maybe she was as affected by their nearness to each other as he was? God, he hoped so!

"I can smell dinner," she said, pointing to the bag he'd set down on the hall table. "It smells delicious."

"The deli it's from is really good."

"Why don't we light the candles now?"

"Good idea."

She struck a match, and he saw her hand tremble slightly as she lit the Shamash first. Then she took that, the main candle, and lit the first and second ones on the menorah.

He liked standing close to her, smelling her perfume, hearing her recite the Hebrew prayer in her musical voice along with his deeper tone. It made the candle-lighting feel intimate rather than just something-to-do.

A glance showed that she'd already set the kitchen table, and after she blew out the match, he followed her into the kitchen, where they warmed the brisket, glazed carrots and potato latkes in the microwave before sitting down. Roslyn had set out both sour cream and applesauce for the latkes. She knew he liked sour cream on his potato pancakes, while she preferred apple sauce.

They started to eat. "This is delicious," she said, cutting more of her potato latke. "Good choice." She chewed for a moment, then drank some soda.

"Glad you like it." He cut more of the brisket, which had a sauce containing onions and spices he didn't recognize.

"You know, Ben," she said, her eyes meeting his, "I think this is the first time you left work early to come here."

"Really?" Was she correct? There were a lot of times he'd come to her place after work. Thinking back, he realized he'd always gotten there late because of the commute. And sometimes left to go back to his apartment and sleep alone, so he didn't have to get up too early the next morning. "I guess you didn't like it when I got here late?" *Way to go, idiot, of course she didn't.* Although she never complained. But then Roslyn wasn't a complainer.

"No, it annoyed me," she answered. "But—I knew how important your job was to you, Ben. How you wanted to make a name for yourself, and not depend on your father's reputation as a lawyer."

"Yes," he agreed. She knew all about that. He stopped eating, and reached over to cover her small hand with his larger one. "I'm sorry., Roslyn. I should have been more considerate. I should have—done this before." His voice dropped.

As her eyes met his, the warmth flowing through his hand clasping hers increased.

Roslyn withdrew her hand and asked him about some of the projects he was working on now. Before he knew it, they finished their meal and were clearing the dishes, then heading out for the Menorah lighting.

The temple lawn was crowded. Today's temperature hadn't been too bad for December, but once night fell it always got colder, so they both bundled up with heavy jackets, hats and gloves. Roslyn also added a scarf.

It was a short drive to the temple nearby, and after parking in the lot, he took Roslyn's hand and led her to the front of the building, where a giant menorah was prominently placed. They stood with the other people and after a few minutes the Rabbi called up a board member to do the honors. As she lit the lights for the second night—flicking a switch at the back of the Menorah, she chanted the traditional blessing.

They all joined in, and Ben enjoyed the sweet tones of Roslyn's voice.

He placed his hands on her shoulders. She leaned into him, and for the first time, he felt hope course through him. She seemed okay with being close. He tightened his grip slightly.

A tremor went through her. She looked back at him and met his eyes.

She felt it too! This magic that seemed to spark between him and her when they were close together. "Roslyn," he whispered as the blessing ended.

But then she stepped forward, and his hands fell to his sides.

He didn't want to rush her—but she felt so good close to him--

"Roz?" A masculine voice called from nearby, as the Rabbi and the board member moved back to join the rest of the crowd. People began to speak and shake hands.

A man with light brown hair approached them.

Roslyn straightened. "Hi, Aaron."

Ben frowned. The other man was as tall as him, with lighter coloring, and a very youthful face. He suspected he was older than he appeared.

Aaron glanced from Roslyn to him and back again. "Roz?" He frowned.

"Aaron, this is Ben Jaffee. Ben, Aaron Jacobs."

Ben shook hands, sizing the guy up. He liked Roslyn, he could see, and suspected the man was disappointed that she was here with him.

He slid closer to Roslyn.

Aaron raised his eyebrows.

Roslyn turned to regard Ben. "Aaron's grandmother is in Sunny Horizons, where I work," she said, rather defensively, Ben thought.

Then she turned more towards Aaron. "Ben is— an old friend."

"Oh." Aaron appeared to be sizing him up.

"More than a friend, actually," Ben said.

"Roslyn?" a female voice called, interrupting them.

Ben caught the relief on her face. Apparently, she didn't want to get stuck between him and Aaron.

At the same time, he heard Aaron whisper "my grandmother told me you weren't seeing anyone."

"I'm not," she whispered back. "Not—exactly."

The woman approaching them looked vaguely familiar. Ben focused on her after shooting Aaron an unfriendly look.

Aaron was doing the same.

Ben smirked. *She's mine.*

"Hi Helen!" Roslyn said, stepping forward and giving the woman a hug.

Belatedly Ben realized the woman was a relative. He vaguely recalled she and her husband had two boys, a little older than Roslyn and her siblings, and they lived in the area.

"Ben, you remember my mother's cousin Helen? Helen, this is Ben Jaffe, an old—friend." She stumbled over the words. "And Aaron Jacobs, a new friend."

Aaron glared at Ben before reaching out to shake hands with Roslyn's cousin, and her husband who approached too.

Ben greeted both Helen and her husband like old friends. "Good to see you again. How are your boys?" he asked. *Take that, Aaron.*

"Oh, fine," Helen said, her eyes going from Ben to Aaron. Her husband Henry smiled at everyone. "You know our youngest, Sam, is getting married in the spring," Helen added.

He'd forgotten. He glanced at Roslyn. Her eyes were steady on Helen. Would the idea that another person in her family was engaged irritate her when he'd been slow to commit? He couldn't read Roslyn's expression.

Helen shivered. "We need to go. I'm cold," she told her husband. "Please come visit us soon!" she said to Roslyn

"I will," Roslyn agreed.

"Nice to meet you," Aaron called after them as they departed.

"Nice to see you again," Ben said simultaneously.

Roslyn turned back to the two of them. "Aaron, stop by my office next time you come to see your grandmother. Ben, please take me home now. I'm cold too."

He wondered if it was an excuse. Roslyn usually didn't mind the cold.

He shot Aaron a triumphant look before saying, "Nice to meet you," to the other man. Grasping her elbow, he led Roslyn away from the crowd, towards the parking lot.

They were almost at his car before she spoke. "We're not exclusive any more. I have a right to meet other men."

He swallowed. "Yes," he said carefully. The last thing he wanted was to get her angry. "But you said you'd give me the eight days of Hanukkah to give us another chance. To convince you we can work."

"I did." He thought he heard a soft sigh.

Was she regretting her decision? Pain twisted his gut.

No. He had to have another chance. He had to.

CHAPTER III

Third Night of Hanukkah

"Hello, Mom." Roslyn leaned back in her office chair as she took the call from her mother.

"Roslyn, sweetie, how are you?"

Most people called her Ros, but her mother—who had named her after an adored grandmother—always used her full name. As did Ben, since he always said it was a beautiful and feminine name.

"I'm fine," she replied automatically. Actually, she'd been in turmoil since last night. Ben—or a chance at a new romance with Aaron? Which was the right choice? Could she see them both?

"My cousin Helen called me last night."

Uh oh. Roslyn could just imagine why. "I ran into her yesterday." Might as well get it out in the open. "At the Menorah lightning at her temple."

"She said you were with *Ben*?"

Her parents knew she had broken it off with him. "Yes," she answered. "He pleaded with me for another chance, so I decided to see what happens."

There was a moment of charged silence. Then, "we don't want you to end up like your Aunt Ann."

She sighed. Her parents had always liked Ben;

but her mother had concerns stemming from the Aunt Ann history. "I know, Mom. And I *won't*. If our relationship doesn't work over Hanukkah, I'm going to kiss him goodbye." She changed the topic to her parent's Hanukkah celebration over the weekend. "What can I bring to your Hanukkah party?"

"Bring a dessert," her mother said. "And—bring Ben. I want to see how he acts towards you now."

So do I. It might be a good idea for her to observe how he acted towards her at a family occasion, now that he had only a few days left to persuade her he was sincere. "Okay," she agreed.

They spoke for a few minutes more, than she got off, knowing she had to prepare for another meeting with a patient's family.

She got out of work promptly at five, for a change, then drove to Ben's condo. He'd begged her last night before he left her apartment to come to his place for this evening's dinner. She thought he wanted to do something to impress her—maybe cook?

The drive was familiar. She could see lights twinkling across the Hudson as she drew closer to Ben's home in Jersey City. She'd always liked the hustle and bustle of the area but was happy to return to her quieter home. They had discussed Ben's preference for a quieter atmosphere, too, in the past. They'd agreed that someday they both wanted to live in the suburbs.

But would they be living together? Or would she be with someone else… someone like Aaron? She dreaded starting to date again. All her single friends were telling her how difficult it was to find someone, even with the popular internet dating sites. And the thought of someone else—she knew she'd miss Ben, terribly, if she spent time with other guys.

Parking was always a problem and she had to pull into the expensive parking garage near his home. Once she walked the block to the building in the blustery cold air, with rain spattering her face, she used the intercom in his modern apartment building.

"Roslyn?" His voice echoed through the entryway.

"Yes."

"I'm buzzing you in." The sound of the buzzer rang through the small vestibule and she grasped the handle and pulled the inner door open.

She took the elevator up to the sixth floor. As she exited and walked down the carpeted hallway, she heard a door open. Ben was waiting in his doorway when she rounded the corner of the hall.

"Hi, Roslyn," he said. He wore a huge grin and his eyes sparkled. "Thanks for coming here!" As she drew close he bent and cupped her face with his hands, giving her a hard kiss.

Even that swift kiss had her insides melting.

"C'mon in. How are you?" He indicated she should proceed him.

"Tired. It was a long day." She shrugged out of her coat.

He grabbed it and hung it up. "Well, now you can relax. Want a glass of wine?"

She hesitated. She'd love one, actually, but she had to drive home and since she was tired, it wasn't a good idea. She shook her head. "No thanks."

"I'm cooking for you." He beamed.

Her mouth nearly dropped open. "Really? What?"

Ben rarely cooked, although he could do some basics.

"Steak and baked potatoes. And I picked up ready-made salad and added a few vegetables."

"I'm impressed." She dropped onto his comfy sectional and kicked off her shoes. She was impressed. He must be trying to please her.

"I wanted to do something for you," he said seriously.

She sat back, looking around his condo. The vast, high-ceilinged rooms with their view of New York City were industrial/modern and gorgeous, and Ben kept it from looking cold with plenty of photos—many of her—and paintings by his cousin Nathan, who was an artist.

"Dinner sounds perfect."

"Want a soda?"

"Yes." She watched him across the kitchen island as he opened the refrigerator. He wore a nice shirt and jeans, and as he bent forward, she saw his muscles move. He really was muscular and masculine, and a part of her yearned to run her hands up his body.

She quickly squashed that thought. She was not here to have sex, as tempting as that thought was. She was here to give him another chance.

He got her her favorite diet cola and took a beer for himself from the fridge. Then he picked up two potatoes, pierced them, and set them in the microwave. "How about we light the menorah now, while the broiler warms up?" he asked, turning to face her.

"Sure." She stood and, in her socks, walked to the counter where a modern stainless steel menorah stood.

"Do you remember helping me buy this?" he asked softly.

"Of course." She liked shopping, and had been

happy to help Ben buy the menorah when he first moved into his condo. At the same time, she could remember wondering if he felt he needed his own because he might not be sharing hers in the future. She had pushed aside that thought.

Now, though, she gave it some consideration. If they were living together and married, they'd only need one. Although some families had more than one, her parents had only had their old brass one plus a hanging felt one for their children when they'd been too little to handle lit candles.

Ben lit the shamash. He stood close as they chanted the prayer together. At the end of the Hebrew words, he put a hand on her shoulder and squeezed lightly.

***

Ben studied Roslyn as they finished the prayer, and he placed the Shamash in its holder.

She had circles under her eyes. Guilt crept through him. Was she losing sleep over him? He hoped not.

"I have something for you." He took the small package from the corner of the kitchen counter and handed it to her.

"You don't have to keep getting me gifts. I don't have anything for you," she pointed out.

"I want to," he said simply.

She tore open the paper to find the Scottish historical romance he'd picked out for her, by one of her favorite authors. "Thank you! I love her books."

"I've seen you reading her books a lot," he said. "I hope you don't have this one already."

"No. It's her newest, and I keep forgetting to go on line and order it."

He smiled, pleased. Impulsively he picked up her hand, kissed it. She smiled briefly. At least she didn't protest his kissing her.

"You better check the steaks again," she suggested, withdrawing her hand.

Disappointment that she'd pulled back so quickly pinged through him. Maybe he was moving too fast. He checked the meat, and asked her about her day.

"One of our patients tried to leave. We caught her, of course," Roslyn said. "She has a broken hip and even with the walker is having trouble getting around. She needs several more weeks of therapy before she's ready to return home."

"I'm sure you explained that to her."

"I did, and so did her doctor and her daughters. But she isn't listening." She sighed.

"You feel bad about what happened," he said, watching her serious expression. She'd always been compassionate.

"Yes. We try to make everyone's stay pleasant, but this patient really wants to go home."

He checked the steaks one more time, and saw they were ready. Roslyn helped him put out the salad, dressing, and the potatoes. He watched her as she did. Even sharing mundane tasks with her was a wonderful thing. He'd never felt that way about anyone else.

"I like doing simple things with you," he blurted.

She met his eyes. "I do too," she whispered.

***

Roslyn swallowed. Had it been a mistake to admit how she liked doing routine things with Ben?

From the first, they'd always seemed in sync. Like a couple. And even though their relationship was now strained, she still had that glimmer of working as a team that had always been present between her and Ben.

They sat down to eat, and talked some more about her day. She asked about his, and he shared that he was working on a difficult contract.

"This is delicious!" she said after chewing the steak.

He grinned. "I seasoned it with a little garlic powder. I remember a chef doing that on that cooking show we watch sometimes."

"I'm impressed even more," she said.

Ben smiled.

A sharp zing of desire moved through Roslyn. Ben's smile, his masculine, citrusy cologne, his broad shoulders—all added up to leave her with a little ache. She missed him. Seeing him like this, reminded her of all the hugs and kisses she found herself missing every day.

Her phone pinged, startling her. "Oh no, I hope she didn't try escaping again! They said they'd let me know if she was agitated." She had thought Mrs. Perlman was calmed down, but left instructions for the nurses to call her if there was an emergency. "Excuse me." She grabbed her purse, and dug for her phone.

"Hope everything's okay," Ben said.

She frowned as she saw the weather alert. "Uh oh, it's sleeting in Franklin. I got an alert from the weather service."

As she said that, sleet struck the big picture window in his condo. Ben frowned too.

"Maybe I better leave now, before it gets worse," she said.

His frown deepened. "You don't have four-wheel drive. The roads could get messy."

"That's why I better leave now."

"Stay here."

Startled, she met his eyes. "Stay here?" Her voice squeaked.

He nodded. "I know you don't want to—fool around when things are so—awkward between us right now." He took a deep breath, as if he'd had trouble getting those words out. "But you can sleep in the bedroom, and I'll pull out the sofabed in my home office."

"But I have work tomorrow—"

"I'll wake you up early enough to get to work," he said. "Hopefully it will clear up in the morning. Besides, you still have some clothes here. One of those outfits should be okay for work."

It was true, she'd always left a few changes of clothes in his place, and he'd done the same with his clothes in her rental. "Let me see."

She went to the closet in the second bedroom, the one Ben used as a home office. Sure enough, she had three outfits there, two of them suitable for work. As she looked, more sleet struck musically against the window. It would be a tough ride home.

"Alright," she agreed as Ben came up behind her.

"I'm glad. I'd worry about you if you drove in this," he said.

They returned to their meal. "I really like everything," She said. "You did a good job."

He smiled. "I promise, I'll cook more often for you, Roslyn."

Pleasure at his words wove through her.

They cleaned up the meal together. He offered her wine again, and this time she took him up on the offer. Sipping a mellow red wine, she watched as he brought out a pumpkin pie.

"From the bakery down the street." He cut two generous pieces.

It was too early to go to sleep after dessert, so she suggested they watch a little TV. While looking at the guide they stumbled on a Hanukkah cartoon program they'd both watched as kids. Roslyn felt a little stiff as she sat next to Ben. He'd placed his arm on the couch behind her. But as the show progressed, she found herself laughing and relaxing. He moved his arm to hold her, and automatically, she leaned into him.

She'd missed this. It was wonderful to sit next to him, surrounded by his warm arm, his slightly spicy aftershave. She snuggled closer as they watched the antics of the babies and toddlers in the cartoon.

Afterwards, Ben suggested watching his favorite basketball team, the Knicks, and she agreed. They remained in the same position, reminding Roslyn of how often they had watched basketball together, and the many games Ben had taken her to.

"I have tickets for the game a couple of days after Christmas," he announced. "I hope you'll go with me, Roslyn."

She'd always enjoyed those live games. But… what if she decided to break up with him. "We'll see," she said coolly.

Disappointment flashed over his face.

"I know we haven't been to a show for over a year," he said slowly, as if the thought had just occurred to him. "Maybe I can get tickets to something you'd like to see—a musical—for the following weekend."

"I'd like that," she said, "if—if we're still together."

He sent her a sad look. Then he gripped her shoulder. "I'm hoping we will be," he said, his voice dropping.

She didn't answer. She sat there, considering. Ben *did* seem to be making a real effort to please her, to woo her. But… was it enough? If she agreed to keep seeing him, would he instantly go back to the way things were—exclusive dating with no commitment?

She worried about that. As the game went on and the Knicks kept scoring, it didn't hold her attention. The other team was playing badly. She found herself yawning. "I hope you don't mind if I go to sleep soon." It was only 10:15, but she was weary and had to get up early.

Besides, she might have trouble sleeping all alone in that comfy king-sized bed of Ben's, without Ben's body next to hers.

"No problem." He stood up. "You have a nightgown in my dresser."

She remembered the dark blue one she kept here, in case she forgot to bring another. It was slinky and wouldn't keep her very warm, but at least the condo was warm and Ben had a thick comforter on the bed.

So many nights she had cuddled in his arms, and his body heat and loving had kept her warm. Kept her hot.

"Thanks." She got up hastily and headed for the bedroom. Grabbing the nightgown and fresh underthings that were beside it, she hurried into the master bath and shut the door.

She trusted him to behave like a gentleman. He'd never been anything but.

As she stepped under the spray of water, she

couldn't help remembering all the times they had showered together, and ended up making love right here.

***

Ben tried not to visualize Roslyn naked, the water sluicing over her.

It was almost impossible.

And just as impossible to stop remembering the times they'd made love in the shower.

He channel-surfed on the TV, trying not to think of the beautiful woman not too far away. The basketball game had ended, the Knicks killing their opponents. He found a hockey game featuring the Toronto Maple Leafs and settled in to watch that.

A few minutes later, her heard the water turn off. Shortly after that Roslyn called out "goodnight." He noticed the book he'd given her was no longer on the coffee table. She must have taken it into the bedroom.

"Goodnight," he answered. He got up and made up the bed in the guestroom/office, glancing at the menorah where the candles had long since burnt out. He hoped their love hadn't been extinguished like the candles.

No. He would convince her to give him this chance.

As sleet struck the window more forcibly, he was glad, very glad, she wasn't driving home in this. She had a small car and was safer here.

He was not quite ready to sleep, and super conscious of the beautiful woman sleeping in his bed. So he spent some time on his computer, emailing a couple of friends to see how they were, checking a website about Israeli politics and another about

37

business. Finally, feeling like he could doze off, he changed into the long-sleeved T-shirt and long flannel boxers he'd removed from the dresser earlier and got ready for bed.

He turned out the lights in the livingroom, but left the nightlight in the kitchen on, in case she woke up and needed to see where she was going.

Ben stared at the closed master bedroom door, and swallowed. And in that moment, he knew something.

He didn't just miss making love to Roslyn in his big bed. He missed holding her, cuddling close with her. He missed sleeping with her.

If they were married, he'd be able to hold her in his arms every night for the rest of his life.

Which was exactly what he was going to do.

CHAPTER IV

Fourth Night of Hanukkah

"Wake up, sleeping beauty." Ben's voice reached her through her dream.

She'd never been a morning person, but the aromatic coffee brew that beckoned her had her sitting up in bed. "Coming," she said. Then yawned.

Scraps of her dream surrounded her. She'd been walking hand in hand with Ben. They were approaching her family's temple.

She ran into the bathroom, then dressed hastily. When she emerged from the bedroom, Ben stood with a mug of coffee in the kitchen. He was already dressed for work, and his hair shown with drops of water. He must have showered in the second bathroom so as not to wake her up. "Here," he said, handing her the mug.

"Thanks!" She sniffed the rich aroma.

"It's clear outside," he said, waving at the large window. "You should have an easy ride back."

She found instant oatmeal in his pantry, and made herself some while he ate his favorite breakfast cereal.

Ben didn't speak much as she ate and sipped coffee. He knew she wasn't very talkative until she'd had at least one cup. "I'm going to have my second cup at work, and get on the road before the worst of the traffic begins," she told him.

"Of course."

"Thank you for such a nice dinner and the book," she said as she put her coat on.

"You're welcome." He stepped forward and helped her, then enveloped her in a hug. "I'm looking forward to seeing you tonight."

"Me too." The words came out before she could stop them.

As she rode the elevator down, she knew they were true. She *was* looking forward to another evening with Ben. More than she had anticipated when she'd said she'd give him this last chance.

She arrived at work early and plunged into her paperwork. The day passed quickly, with meetings and preparations for the holiday party for the patients.

Since she'd worked through most of her lunch hour, Roslyn left work a few minutes early. She battled traffic on the main road but once she turned off it, traffic was light. She arrived home and had time to change to jeans and a burgundy sweater. She added the earrings and necklace from Ben and left out the book he'd given her, a favorite bookmark stuck inside it.

She'd fought with herself today, Ben foremost in her thoughts. Should she stay with him? Should she break up? She didn't like that he had discouraged Aaron the other night. Yet last night, he'd been so considerate, and she'd felt so good snuggled against him on the couch.

What should she do? She felt pulled in two directions and didn't like the feeling at all. She usually was never this indecisive.

Memories of all their good times together

bombarded her as she took out the ingredients for supper. How she would clutch his arm during a scary suspense movie. Swimming with him at a weekend down the shore. Walking on a snowy evening.

But, fears hit her too. Fears of ending up like her aunt. Or worse, her cousin.

She made chicken with a sauce and prepped for a rice pilaf dish. Once she'd gotten the chicken in the oven, she brushed her hair and was applying fresh lip gloss when her bell rang. It was only a few minutes after five. That couldn't be him, already, could it?

She looked through the peephole. It was.

"Come in," she said as she opened the door. "I didn't expect you so early."

"I worked a half day today and took Thursday and Friday off," he said.

Her astonishment must have shown on her face as shock vibrated through her body. He was usually married to his job, reluctant to take days off even when he didn't feel good.

"You took time off?"

"For you."

For her? Wow. Just… wow.

"I—can't believe it," she murmured. She stepped aside and he entered the hall. "Thank you."

"Believe it," he said firmly. For a moment, a grim expression crossed his handsome face. "I should do this more often. I have a lot of time off accumulated." He seized her hand and squeezed.

She felt her insides melting. He had taken time off—for her. For no other reason. She swallowed, absurdly touched.

Maybe, he really was changing.

He sniffed the air as he took off his coat. "Do I smell your chicken with apricot sauce?"

"Bingo," she said.

"Yum!" He rubbed his hands together.

She smiled as he followed her into the living room.

"Want some wine?" she asked.

"No thanks. But I could use a cup of coffee."

She made him coffee as they talked about work. Then she made the rice and basted the chicken.

"Need any help?" he asked, sipping his coffee.

Ben had always been willing to help others, but he generally didn't do much cooking—except for last night.

She met his eyes. "You really are trying to show me you've changed."

"Absolutely," he said. He put his mug down, and when she stopped stirring the rice, grabbed her hand. "I want you back, Roslyn. I want to prove that."

She hesitated, then admitted in a low voice, "you're doing a good job, Ben."

His eyes widened. "Am I really?"

"Y-yes."

He pulled her closer. "I intend to keep doing that." And he gave her a hard kiss.

She clutched him, and he held her tightly. For a few seconds they said nothing. Then, she loosened her grip. She wasn't ready to go too far at this point. Admitting out loud that he might be persuading her to take him back was further than she'd meant to go.

Stepping back, she said, "Dinner should be ready soon."

"Why don't we light the menorah?" he asked.

Today Roslyn's hands were steady as she touched

the Shamash to the candles. When she put it in its place, Ben, who'd stood beside her, whispered "Happy Hanukkah," his breath feathering over her cheek.

"Happy Hanukkah," she responded.

"I have another gift for you."

She felt like rolling her eyes. "I told you, you don't have to get me something every night."

"And I told you, I want to." His voice was firm. He handed her a gift bag full of tissue paper.

Maybe she should consider getting him something one night, she thought as she opened the bag. Like, for the last night of Hanukkah.

She removed a silver-toned frame. In it was a photo from her cousin's Bar Mitzvah four years ago— of her dancing with Ben. They were smiling as they gazed into each other's eyes.

She gasped. "How—"

"The photographer took a lot of candid shots. I called your uncle and asked if there was one of the two of us. There was, and he emailed me a copy which I printed. I thought it would remind you of how we met."

Tears welled in her eyes. The day they'd met, captured in a photo. She could still remember that giddy feeling when she'd met Ben, the flare of attraction between them. He'd asked her out when the party was winding down.

"Thank you," she said to him now, her voice wobbling. "This is—very thoughtful."

"I want to remind you of how we met, and fell for each other right away," he admitted.

She met his eyes, and a frisson of excitement swam up her spine.

It was still there. This—zing between them.

***

Ben caught sight of the sheen in Roslyn's eyes.

The photograph had touched her. Just as he'd hoped it would. It had reminded her of how they met, their tremendous attraction to each other, and the exciting weeks that followed as they'd dated, come to know each other, and eventually shared passion-filled nights.

But he hated that it had brought her to tears. He gently wiped away one that slid down her cheek.

"I never meant to make you cry," he whispered.

She laughed shakily. "I did enough of that recently."

"I'm so sorry." He cupped her head with his hands. "I can't stand to see you cry, Roslyn."

She stepped back abruptly. "Then—don't give me a reason."

"I'm trying." He paused. "Do you see that?"

She nodded. "I can see. But whether or not you've changed… " her voice drifted off.

"I have." He said it firmly.

She looked at him again. "I'm not sure."

"I'm trying to convince you. You said you'd give me this chance."

He almost didn't catch her soft sigh. "I am giving you a chance," she said quietly. "uhm… let's eat now, okay?"

He went along with the change of focus, wondering if she was a little embarrassed by her strong reaction to the photo.

She was a good cook, and he savored every bite of the delicious chicken and rice. Afterwards, he helped her clean up and stack the dishwasher. He suggested watching a movie they both liked, and they settled on the couch together to watch the original "Ghostbusters." They'd watched it together plenty of times, but it never failed to entertain. Ben put his arm around her and Roslyn moved closer as she always had. A good sign, he thought.

As the movie went on, he pulled her closer, and she rested her head on his shoulder. If they could be like this every night, he'd be happy.

Roslyn snuggled closer, thinking how comfortable she always felt with Ben. Even if they were doing something mundane like watching a movie at home.

But they were back into their routine. Had Ben truly changed? Or was he just as scared of marriage as he'd always been?

When the music blared, signaling the end, and the world was saved, Ben gently kissed the top of her head.

She looked up, and saw a look of yearning on his face that was so strong she caught her breath.

He wanted her. But she knew it was too soon. She was too uncertain for more than a kiss right now.

"I guess I better go," he said, reluctance in his voice.

"Yes. Tomorrow's a work day for me," Roslyn replied.

As she walked him to the door, she was bombarded with images of them in her bed, making love or simply cuddling.

Would that happen again? Would she want it to?

CHAPTER V

Fifth Night of Hanukkah

Ben left his condo way before the traffic started. He didn't want to arrive at Roslyn's before she got home, so he decided to stop at a mall. He spent an hour there, picking up gifts for his sister, his father, and even his stepmother.

He and Harriet, his father's second wife, had, after many years of friction, settled into a congenial but very superficial relationship. He'd realized years ago that he would never change his cheating father or sly stepmother. Or his sad, depressed mother.

The weirdest thing was that his stepmother liked to pretend they were one big, happy Brady-bunch combined family.

His brother had gotten used to the whole idea after a few years, quicker than he had. His step-sister had too. He and his stepbrother had bonded over their anger and disgust about their parents' affair and subsequent marriage. Acceptance had taken years.

Ben pulled into the mall parking lot now, and exited the car. He already had a present for Roslyn for tonight: funny Hanukkah socks, decorated with dreidels and menorahs.

Now he needed three more gifts, so this would give him an hour to shop for just the right presents.

He wandered around the mall. He was tempted to go into the British lingerie store, but he knew he'd want to buy a whole bunch of things for Roslyn, and he was pretty sure that she didn't want to make love while she was considering his request to get back with her.

So… what to get her?

He walked around, eyeing different window displays. A beautiful red sweater caught his eye in one of the women's stores. Nothing very original in buying a sweater, but… the color would look great on his Roslyn, with her dark hair and eyes.

Once he'd seen it close up, he realized that it would mold her beautiful breasts, and he whipped out his charge card to pay for it. Fingering the soft fabric, he could imagine how it would feel to skim his hands over her when she wore it. Just the thought had his member twitching.

After he purchased the sweater, he retreated hastily form the store, and stopped to get a soda and a pretzel. After finishing, he glanced at his watch, and saw it was still too early to head to Roslyn's.

He was strolling past a jewelry store when he caught sight of its sign: "Getting engaged for the holidays?" Engagement rings were prominently displayed in the window, along with a Christmas stocking and Hanukkah menorah.

His footsteps slowed.

Of course.

He'd planned from the beginning that he would propose on the last night of Hanukkah. And then they could shop for ring.

But it would be more meaningful if he gave Roslyn the symbol of his love and devotion, the concrete proof that he wanted to marry her when he *did* propose. The proof he should have given her a couple of years ago.

He stared at the different shapes and sizes of diamonds and other stones which were on display.

He knew Roslyn liked classic styles of rings from remarks she'd made about her friends' rings. She'd also fawned over his cousin Jessica's ring two years ago. He was certain he saw one with the exact same shape in the window.

He strode into the store.

"May I help you?" A gray-haired, distinguished gentleman asked.

"I'd like to see engagement rings. Like those in the window."

The man asked him a few questions about styles and his price range. Fortunately, Ben had money saved. He knew diamonds weren't cheap.

He studied a few, then asked for the specific one that had caught his eye. "My girlfriend likes that shape," he told the salesman.

The salesman brought it over and let Ben examine it. "It's a marquis shaped ring, with the two baguettes. It's a little over one carat," the man explained. "And the color and clarity are excellent."

He named the price, which was expensive, but Ben had the money and knew Roslyn was worth every penny.

"I'll take it," he said. "What if it doesn't fit?"

"You can bring it back with her and we'll be glad to resize the ring," the man said.

Feeling happy and a little nervous with the

purchase, Ben pulled out his credit card and bought the ring. He asked the salesman to hold onto it while he finished his shopping.

The ring was for night number eight. He had tonight and night number six covered. Now for number seven…

He wandered around some more, and stopped at a candle shop. Roslyn liked those candles in a jar. He went in selecting a few to sniff. He finally picked one with a tropical scent. Roslyn had always said she wanted to visit Hawaii.

Hopefully, on their honeymoon, he decided. Warm beaches, loads of flowers, tropical sunsets… it sounded perfect.

Once he had that package, he returned and picked up the ring. The salesman congratulated him and gave him some gold wrap to cover the velvet box. Ben checked the ring again, then snapped the box shut and pocketed it.

It took him more than a half hour to get to Roslyn's home, since traffic was building up on the highway now.

When he arrived at her condo complex, he carefully tucked the box with the ring in the glove compartment of his car, and locked up.

He felt like skipping up the steps to her front door. He resisted the impulse, keeping to a quick walk instead. He'd bought her a ring! He would marry the love of his life!

What if she doesn't want to? A little voice in his head asked.

He stopped.

Of course she'd want to. Right? She wanted to get married.

And at that moment, realization zapped him.

This is how Roslyn feels. Unsure if he, Ben, would want to marry her.

He swallowed, clutching the bag with tonight's gift as the revelation ricocheted through his entire being. He understood, finally, what she felt. Uncertainty. Nervousness. Confusion.

He never wanted her to feel that way again! He'd make sure of it!

He would do anything to take that fear, that uncertainty, away from the love of his life.

Marriage no longer seemed like such a gamble. It would mean making sure the woman he loved was happy and had the stability of his love. Always.

He started back up to her door, his footsteps firm. She opened the door the minute he rang the bell.

"Hi, Ben." She looked beautiful, wearing a gray sweater tunic over black leggings and boots. He wanted to lick his lips, she looked so appealing.

"Hi. You look great." He pulled her into his arms and gave her a smacking kiss on the lips.

When she pulled away, she was smiling. "Thanks. C'mon in. Give me your coat."

He shrugged out of his coat, then followed her into the livingroom. She hung the coat in a closet and he smelled last night's dinner in the air. She gave him an appraising look. "You look good too."

He was glad he'd worn his new jeans with a nice shirt and sweater.

"We have leftovers," she said, "plus I made a big, healthy salad to go with the chicken, and some rolls."

"I'll take your leftovers any time," he said. "You're such a good cook, I never mind if we have them."

They sat on the couch and he asked about her day. Apparently today had been a little easier for her. Tomorrow, Friday, they were having a Hanukkah/Christmas/Kwanzaa party at her workplace for the residents, and she was going to get dressed up for that.

"Because of the party, I won't have any meetings with families, so it will be a relaxing day for me," she told him. "I have to get to work early; but I can leave early."

"Let's go out to that Chinese restaurant you like so much," he suggested. "The one we ate in when I told you I wanted to have an exclusive relationship with you, and you agreed. Or, would you rather go there on Saturday?"

She shook her head. "Saturday afternoon is my parent's Hanukkah celebration. So Saturday night I'd rather have a quiet evening." She met his look squarely. "You're invited too. Do you want to come?"

Of course he did! "Yes," he declared.

"They do know that I wanted to break up with you," she said.

Disappointment pinged inside him. He should have guessed she'd say something to her family. "They do?"

"Yes, but I told them I'm giving you a second chance." She shrugged, and smiled slightly.

"I want that second chance," he said firmly. He reached out and grasped her hand. "I love you, Roslyn." He'd said it before, but he hoped that now, the words would have extra meaning.

She looked at him, her eyes sad.

"Just—not enough," she whispered.

"That's not true." Desperation clawed at him. "I do love you. Enough for *everything*." He hoped that emphasizing the last word would give her a clue. He wanted to make a grand gesture with the ring, on the last night of Hanukkah. To give her the tangible proof of his love and devotion.

For a moment, he was tempted to propose then and there. But he knew that waiting for the eighth night of Hanukkah—the last night--would be the most dramatic. And he hoped she'd revel in that excitement.

She moved away. "We'll see. It's hard to believe that, even though you've been so sweet the last few nights," she stated. "I won't make up my mind until the eighth night of Hanukkah. I promised I'd give you that chance."

The eighth night. Perfect.

"Yes. And I appreciate it." He swallowed. What more could he say? "Should we light the menorah now?"

"Sure." Her voice was nonchalant, too, but he suspected it was an act.

After they lit the candles and chanted the prayer, he handed her the gift-wrapped socks. Tearing open the package, she started to laugh. "Hanukkah socks! How cute." At least she seemed genuinely happy now.

He grinned. "I thought you'd get a kick out of them."

"I do." She placed them on a side table. "Are you ready to eat?"

They ate dinner, and he managed to keep the conversation lighter, telling amusing stories about some of his coworkers. After dinner they cleaned up, and he suggested a game of scrabble.

They were both good with words, but Roslyn won using the Q for "quickly." He won the second game with "zany."

"I know you have to get to work early. But we'll go to our favorite China Royale tomorrow," he reiterated as he stood up.

"Yes." Smiling, she got him his coat.

He leaned down to kiss her before she opened the door.

She slid her arms around him, and he pulled her in tighter, feeling her against him, even through his thick coat. No one had ever turned him on like Roslyn. Heat flared inside him.

"Roslyn… " he whispered, kissing her hungrily.

She hesitated for just a second, then leaned into him, kissing him back, hard.

Every molecule in his body leapt to attention. He squeezed her closer.

She pulled away. "I'll see you tomorrow, Ben." He heard the tremor in her voice. He hoped she was having as strong a reaction to their kiss as he was.

"Tomorrow." He left, waving as he got to the curb. She was standing in her doorway, watching him.

He continued to his car, knowing he'd dream of her tonight.

***

Roslyn leaned against her door, breathing heavily.

She had been wavering all week about whether to give her relationship with Ben another chance. But when he kissed her—her whole body, her whole being, melted into him.

She'd never, ever had a reaction like that with any other man she'd dated in the past. She knew it wasn't just physical—it was emotional too. No one else had made her so happy, been so considerate on a daily basis.

She caught sight of the menorah, sitting on the table. Three more nights.

What would she do?

CHAPTER VI

Sixth Night of Hanukkah

The Sunny Horizons party finished right on time. After helping with the clean-up and hearing many thank yous and congratulations, Roslyn returned to her office, grabbed her purse and coat, and left the center just before three o'clock.

Once home, she discovered the gift she had ordered on line for Ben had arrived. It was a Hanukkah tie, with multi-colored dreidels in various sizes. She thought Ben would enjoy wearing it since he loved the holiday of Hanukkah.

She checked her make-up carefully. She'd worn a forest green sweater and black skirt with the dreidel earrings and necklace he'd given her. The patients all seemed to enjoy seeing her dressed for the holiday.

Ben was supposed to arrive at four o'clock, so she sat down to relax and read before he did. She was really enjoying the book he'd given her, and reminded herself to tell him so.

Not for the first time, she wondered if he'd try to seduce her this weekend. Or… would she attempt to seduce him? They'd always had a great sexual relationship.

She had deliberately worn one of her sexy, lacy bras and bikinis. Just in case, she told herself. She wondered if making love with Ben would help her make a decision. Would she feel closer, more committed to him? Or would she feel afterwards that nothing had changed, that there was a gap that simply couldn't be overcome?

She tried to shut down the tantalizing images of herself tangled up in the sheets with Ben, and was only partially successful. She reread a page several times before she could immerse herself in the Scottish romance again.

The ringing of her doorbell startled her. She'd lost track of time, and it was already a couple of minutes before four o'clock. Ben was here.

She scrambled out of her chair and went to answer the door.

"Hi." She couldn't prevent the breathless note in her voice.

"Hi." His admiring glance made her cheeks grow warm. He bent to give her a swift kiss.

When he entered the apartment, she felt small beside his height—as usual. And she liked it, as usual.

"It's early for dinner. Should we light the candles before we go out?" she asked.

"Sure."

They lit the candles and chanted the prayer. Then she gave him his gift.

He laughed when he opened the box. "A Hanukkah tie! How cool. I'll wear it now." He wore a nice blue shirt and jeans, and he went to the mirror to put the tie on and get it straight.

She stood near him, admiring his physique, very

conscious of his presence. She breathed in the masculine scent of his woodsy aftershave.

"It looks good on you," she said, glad he liked the gift.

"You look great. You have the dreidel jewelry on, so we match." He reached out and fingered the necklace.

She sucked in her breath, audibly. For a moment they stood there, staring at each other.

Then Ben turned and grabbed a box he'd put down on her hall table, beside the menorah. He handed it to her. "Happy sixth night of Hanukkah."

She tore off the giftwrap and opened it. Nestled inside blue tissue paper decorated with snowflakes was a beautiful red sweater.

"I love it," she said. Ben knew red was one of her favorite colors to wear.

"It will look beautiful on you," he said.

They sat and he asked about her work party. Ben had a party at work coming up the following weekend, and asked her to accompany him.

She hesitated. "If we're still dating," she said.

Disappointment flooded his face. Then, she watched as he struggled to maintain a neutral expression. "Alright. You know I hope we are, Roslyn. I want a permanent relationship with you. I appreciate you're giving me another chance, and I'm not going to blow it."

She shifted her position, uncomfortable. He knew this was an experiment, that they might not end up together. But she was feeling badly now. She could hear in his voice how much he wanted this. Wanted *her*.

Especially since he'd just declared that he had every intention of making it work.

But what was permanent to him? Moving in together? Dating for a long time? Was the M word still difficult for him to commit to?

She wanted to enjoy the evening, not make a decision this minute. Attempting to lighten the atmosphere, she told him a few stories about the patients who had come to the party, the magician who performed for them, and the fun everyone had.

"Except," she added, "a few patients didn't come because they were sleeping—but one in particular simply refuses to participate in anything. She keeps saying she hates it here, and she won't give us a chance." She sighed.

"Isn't there anything you can do?" he asked in his deep baritone.

"I wish. I tried to get her to Bingo, to card games—she just turns up her nose and says she doesn't do any of *those* things. I keep thinking she's lonely inside, but she refuses to come to anything."

"What does her family say?"

"She has three daughters. One lives on the other side of the country, but the other two say their mother has always been that way, thinks she's superior and resents being in rehab. They don't think she'll ever change. She thinks these activities are beneath her. But—I feel like I've failed to help her."

"That's too bad she has that attitude." He picked up her hand and stroked it. "I'm positive you tried, but you can't succeed with everyone."

Tiny sparks seemed to move up her arm at his touch.

He asked her about some of the other patients, and she described a few who were making progress.

Soon afterward, he suggested heading to the restaurant. The candles had already burned out, and they left for dinner.

Wind struck them as they approached the car, and Ben opened the door for Roslyn to slide inside.

Ben's car was spotless—unlike hers; and pretty luxurious feeling. He was a good driver, and even though they were buffeted by the wind, the drive to the restaurant was smooth. She asked him about his co-workers, since she'd met a few of them in the past.

The restaurant they liked was decorated in red and gold, with Chinese lanterns spaced around the room, a tank of large goldfish, and a big brass drum hanging in a corner.

Once there, they were led to a secluded booth and given fragrant tea.

"Do you know what you want to eat?" he asked as they opened the menus.

She shook her head.

They finally decided on chicken with broccoli, sweet and sour chicken, and vegetable fried rice, which they would share. It was a meal they'd had many times here.

After ordering, Ben reached out and grasped her hand in his warm one. "I always like the food here. But the best part is being with you, Roslyn."

"Thank you," she whispered, her insides melting at his words and warm look.

Over their delicious meal, they talked and Roslyn flirted with Ben, touching his hand, smiling up at him, pushing back a lock of his hair. She could feel her resistance to Ben flowing away. She did still care for him. And from the graze of his lips on her hand and the touch of his fingers on her cheek, he wanted very much to keep his relationship with her.

The wind was colder and stronger when they left the restaurant. Ben wrapped his arm around her as he led her to his car. Snowflakes were coming down, not thickly, but enough to dampen their faces.

It reminded her so much of their first date, and how it had been snowing lightly when they'd left that restaurant.

Once they were back at her place she invited him in for a drink. She poured him a scotch and soda. It was his favorite and she kept a bottle of good scotch handy. Then she poured herself a small liqueur glass of amaretto, her favorite.

They sat on her couch and she toed off her pumps. He followed her example with his shoes.

"Oh, that feels good." She wiggled her stockinged feet, sipping her drink. It was strong and sweet and tasted sharply of almonds.

Ben drank from his glass. "Perfect." He clinked his ice cubes, catching the light, and smiled at her. Leaning towards her, he brushed her cheek with his hand.

"I love you," he whispered.

It was exactly what she needed to hear and she made up her mind at that moment. She took both their drinks, placed them on the side table, then slid into his lap. "Ben," she whispered, and wrapping her arms around his neck, kissed him. Hard.

He responded immediately, drawing her closer, his tongue thrusting inside her mouth. She tasted the strong scotch and the more subtle soda. She felt him grow hard under her, and squirmed, applying a friction that turned her on as well as made him harder.

"Roslyn," he moaned, freeing her mouth for a moment. "Roslyn… you have no idea how much I want you."

"I think I have a pretty good idea," she said, massaging his neck with her fingers.

Their tongues danced as she pressed her breasts against him. She wanted him. Wanted him *now*.

His hand brushed her breast, and she immediately felt her nipple peak as her insides tightened in anticipation.

His hand stroked her, and their kiss grew more fiery. Then he slipped it under her sweater, and he caressed her through her lacy bra.

"Roslyn," he breathed.

"B-Ben," she whispered, longing filling her. She kissed him feverishly,

"Roslyn, I want to make love to you. Please tell me you want that too. Let me love you."

"Yes." She wanted, needed Ben.

He stood, and picked her up. Carrying her to her bedroom, he gently laid her on the bed, then covered her body with his own.

The weight of him felt good, so good—she kept kissing him as his hands roved over her. Her body felt alive everywhere he touched and stroked. How she'd missed his caresses!

He pulled off her sweater and stared at her. "You are so beautiful," his whispered, his voice raspy with desire.

She tugged at his tie.

He sat up, rapidly divesting himself of his tie and shirt. She squirmed out of her skirt and pantyhose, until she lay only in her lacy blue bra and bikini. Inhaling his masculine aftershave, she watched as he shed his pants and boxers. His cock sprang forth, and she touched it gently.

"Roslyn." He almost sounded in pain. "I've missed making love to you so much."

He lay down beside her and gathered her close. "You feel so good." He bent his head and swirled his tongue around one nipple, and she felt the wet heat through the lace of her bra. It was totally erotic.

She found herself rubbing against his body. "Ohh... Ben... "

He switched to her other breast, and then unclasped her bra to suck on one nipple, then the other.

And his hand moved, cupping her.

She tightened her legs around his hand as his palm pressed against her.

She wanted him here, in her center.

She felt him pull her panties off as his lips moved down her stomach, kissing her navel, then up to her breast again.

He touched her.

"Ben, she gasped again. She'd never felt such heat, such need for him. Maybe it was the lack of sex for several weeks, maybe it was just that he touched her so reverently. Whatever it was, she wanted him to touch her intimately.

"Yeah, baby? Tell me what you want," he whispered, his voice husky, sending shivers of anticipation through her.

"You. You!"

His finger slipped inside her. She writhed, feeling the pressure build. "I want you now," she gasped.

His finger withdrew, and as she protested, she heard foil tear. Peeking at him, she saw him sheath himself.

"Now, where were we?" He bent over her.

She opened for him, and he thrust inside. She gasped with the pleasure of it, the heaviness of Ben inside her, touching her, exactly where she wanted him. Heat suffused her as he rocked further into her.

"Oh—oh—" she couldn't say a coherent word. She could only feel Ben, deep inside, his heat and length making her wild.

"Roslyn—Roslyn—you feel so good—"

She felt the tension building. She gasped, and then suddenly, as he thrust again, she shattered into a million stars. "Ben!"

And he was right there with her. "Roslyn!"

He collapsed against her. The weight of him, as her spasms continued, felt incredibly good.

After a minute he rolled to the side, taking her with him. "Oh my God, that was incredible," he murmured.

"Hmm hmm." She stroked his hair.

"I missed making love to you." He kissed her, sweetly, his lips tender.

"Me too." She opened her eyes to find him studying her and smiling. "Stay with me tonight?"

"I was hoping you'd ask." He pulled her tightly against him.

She cuddled closer. "I love you," she murmured without thinking.

He tightened his hold. "I love *you*, Roslyn."

For a moment, she panicked. Should she have admitted that? Then as he held her close, his heartbeat pounding against her cheek, she relaxed. Ben. She did love him. She probably always would…

They must have dozed. Gradually she became aware of his breathing, and opened her eyes. He was studying her. "Roslyn." His whisper stirred her hair.

She felt him growing hard against her thigh. She kissed his chest.

"No one turns me on like you," he whispered, and they made love again.

***

During the night, the hissing at her window woke Roslyn. She felt something warm next to her, and turned.

Ben. He was snuggled close, one arm around her, her back to his front. He was breathing slowly and steadily.

Wind rattled the window, and she guessed it was snowing harder outside.

The closeness and warmth she felt lying next to Ben was indescribable. She snuggled closer, and shut her eyes.

She loved this feeling. Wanted to hang on to it.

But… was that the best thing for her peace of mind?

CHAPTER VII

Seventh Night of Hanukkah

When Ben woke, after a fantastic night's sleep, Roslyn had already gotten up and he heard her in the shower.

He lay in bed, thinking. Making love last night with her had been perfect. He couldn't wait to do that again.

She returned to the bedroom, wrapped in a thick pale blue robe. He whistled. "You look sexy even in that robe."

She smiled. "You can use the shower now."

He was tempted to try to lure her back to bed, but he got the feeling she was a little restrained this morning. Was she having morning-after regrets? He hoped not.

He still had the extra clothes he'd always kept at Roslyn's, plus some in the trunk of his car. He went into the walk-in closet, grabbed a shirt, sweater and jeans and proceeded to the bathroom.

Once showered, he peeked out the window. There were about three inches of snow on the ground, just enough to make the day look festive without being too much of a nuisance.

He joined Roslyn in the kitchen. She'd toasted a

couple of bagels and put out cream cheese. The coffee she made smelled good and rich, and he inhaled. "Perfect." He moved behind her, surrounding her with his arms, and kissed the nape of her neck.

She leaned into him. "Are you ready to see my family this afternoon?"

"I'm looking forward to it." He meant it. Roslyn's family was nice, and a lot more functional than his own.

He turned her in his arms. "Last night was wonderful."

A shadow crossed her face. "I—yes." She sounded uncertain.

"I meant it, you know. I love you, Roslyn."

She looked at him, a serious expression on her face. "Ben, last night was special. Very special. But—it doesn't change anything."

His stomach dropped. "What do you mean?"

She regarded him. "I mean, just because we had sex—admittedly mind-blowing sex—doesn't mean I've decided to get back with you after Hanukkah is over."

He swallowed, disappointment echoing in him as if his body was hollow. "I thought—" he began hoarsely.

"I guessed what you thought." She said it gently, but firmly. "We've always been great together in that way. But it doesn't mean I've made up my mind. I still—haven't." Her voice stumbled.

He reached out and caught her hand, stroking his thumb against it. "How can I convince you?"

She shrugged. "I don't know. Let's—see what happens."

He had to be content with that for the time being. But he hoped… he hoped to win her heart.

***

When they got to Roslyn's parents' house, it was noisy, and the smell of home cooked food lured him towards the kitchen.

Her father greeted him as enthusiastically as always. Her mother, though, seemed a little more formal, a little more restrained than her usual happy self, which always reminded him of her daughter.

He was happy to see the Stein's dog, Buddy, a big black mutt who was always friendly. The dog greeted him like a long-lost friend, and he spent time stroking him and sneaked him a couple of milkbones.

He went to greet Roslyn's sister Sarah, who was talking to her boyfriend Adam and a cousin, Emily.

They all greeted him just as cordially as ever, but he noticed Sarah assessing him as they spoke. Sarah was a lawyer, working for her uncle and Ben's father's firm. He felt like she was studying him now. Adam was an attorney too, but he seemed more casual. Ben guessed that Sarah knew about what was going on between him and Roslyn.

As she spoke, Sarah waved her hand and he caught sight of the pear-shaped diamond on her left hand.

"I see congratulations are in order," he said, and kissed her cheek, then pumped Adam's hand. "When did you get engaged?"

"Thanksgiving weekend," Sarah said.

Roslyn had said *nothing* to him about this big event. But now he understood why she'd suddenly assumed that he would never marry her. Sarah and Adam had been going out only a year or so, and they were already engaged.

He should have realized something precipitated Roslyn's actions. How could he be so dumb?

Roslyn must have thought that if he couldn't commit after four years, he never would.

Ben swallowed, bile suddenly rushing up his throat as the truth slammed into him. It was his own fault. He'd dragged things out because of his own insecurities, and Roslyn had felt she had no choice but to break up with him.

He regretted his hesitation, his failure to act.

He managed to get through a brief conversation with Sarah, Adam and Emily. But his mind was racing as he tried his hardest to pay attention to their chatter about Emily's recent trip to Israel.

Eventually he excused himself and drew closer to the stove, where he could see Mrs. Stein stood near her flavorful brisket.

He offered to help cut the meat, but Roslyn's mother shooed him away, insisting her husband could do it. Still, she gave him a tray of latkes and told him to put them on the dining room table, since they'd be serving buffet-style.

He and Roslyn's brother Scott and Roslyn helped set up the table, and before long Roslyn's dad called everyone in to eat. Ben greeted a couple of aunts and uncles and cousins who were here, along with Roslyn's grandmother, who was looking frailer than when he'd seen her last.

He found a seat next to Roslyn in the family room, and dug into the meal. Her mother's brisket was mouth-watering and the potato latkes perfect—nice and crisp. He'd added sour cream on top, and also helped himself to the green beans almondine that were on the table.

"Everything's delicious," he said.

She agreed, but didn't say much else.

Was she, like him, thinking about her sister's engagement?

A little later her mother lit the candles and they all stood together, reciting the prayer. Then, gifts came out and started going the rounds.

He'd brought a bottle of wine for her parents and a toy for her dog, but nothing else. Yet her parents, Sarah and Adam, and Scott all had gifts for him: gift cards to Best Buy, Amazon, and Barnes and Noble. He thanked each person graciously and felt bad that he hadn't brought more.

But Roslyn had—she gave her sister and future brother-in-law a gift card to a popular chain restaurant they liked; and her brother a Best Buy gift card he could use towards a new laptop.

The food was delicious, and the camaraderie warm. He enjoyed Roslyn's family, and was grateful they were treating him the same way they always had. Only Roslyn seemed more subdued, not touching him as often as she usually did, not meeting his eyes quite as much as usual.

And it pierced him to the core.

He was tempted to propose when they left and went back to her place. He had to bite his lip to keep from blurting out the words.

Once back at her place, they shrugged out of their coats, and lit her menorah. He handed her the gift bag with the candle he'd bought.

"Oh, I love these!" She lifted the lid. "Mmm… nice and tropical. I'll light it now."

She did, and the fragrance immediately began to envelope the room.

Roslyn pulled off her boots. "Want a drink?"

He could use one. "Sure." He followed her into the kitchen.

She poured them both wine, and they went to sit on the couch. "Tomorrow I'm meeting my friend Antonia for lunch," she told him. "You've met her— she's my friend from grad school."

"I'll come over at dinner time," he said. "We can go out to eat again."

"Okay." They sat quietly, and he wished he knew exactly what she was thinking.

He reached over and smoothed a hand over her hair. "You're so beautiful, Roslyn. You outshine everyone in your family."

"Thanks."

"I really appreciate that your family is so— accepting of me."

"They've always liked you," she said.

"And I like them. But you—you're the shining star."

She laughed. "I'm sure they wouldn't all agree. Sarah's a successful lawyer and makes a lot of money. My cousin Emily is an art therapist. And my brother is going to be a CPA when he finishes college. I'm just a social worker."

"Not 'just'," he protested, sliding closer.

"You've always been my biggest cheerleader."

"I still am. I love you, Roslyn." He pulled her into his arms.

Their kisses became more heated, and within minutes they headed to her bedroom, where they made love.

CHAPTER VIII

Eighth Night of Hanukkah

Roslyn didn't sleep peacefully that night. She woke several times, aware of the fact that she had to make a momentous decision tonight.

On one hand, when Ben said he loved her she knew he was sincere. And when he touched her and made love to her, she felt as close to him as she always had.

On the other hand, when Sarah had taken her aside yesterday and talked about having Roslyn with her when she shopped for a bridal gown, Roslyn had felt a stab of jealously. She wanted that. And she wasn't convinced she'd get a marriage ring with Ben.

He'd said he loved her, wanted a relationship with her. But enough to marry her?

She slid out of bed quietly, and went to shower.

When she got out Ben was just waking up. "Good morning, beautiful," he said, and grabbing her arm, pulled her down for a resounding kiss.

She sat up after a minute. "I have to get dressed to meet Antonia."

"I know." He stood up, and she eyed his masculine body with appreciation. "I thought I'd ride over to my brother's and see if he wants to go to lunch, too."

An hour later they parted for their destinations. As she drove, Roslyn's feelings ping-ponged. Should she stay with Ben? Should she break up? She had to give him an answer.

When she got to the Thai restaurant which was approximately halfway between their homes, Roslyn found Antonia had just arrived. They were shown a table and opened their menus.

Roslyn had met Antonia in one of her grad school classes at Rutgers, and they'd become friends. Her friend had returned to school after four years in the workplace. She'd discovered a psychology major didn't have much choice of jobs without an advanced degree, and instead of psychology, decided on social work. Now, she worked for a foundation which helped people with developmental disabilities and was happy with her job.

But not her marriage, she confessed.

"We've agreed to separate after the holidays," she said with a sigh. "I should have known going in that it wouldn't work."

"Why?" Roslyn asked. Antonia had been married for over two years.

"Remember when I broke up with my longtime boyfriend, Brad? Well, I was determined to find a guy and settle down." She sighed again, and sipped some tea. "I pursued Jake because I thought he was exactly what I wanted—an educated man, an accountant, he came from a similar background—everything sounded good. But within a year of our wedding, the spark fizzled out. We just don't have a deep, abiding love." She met Roslyn's eyes.

Roslyn felt sad. She'd been at Antonia's wedding, had thought she and Jake were a good match.

"I should have stuck with Brad," Antonia continued. "He got married a year ago, and he and his wife are expecting twins. I realized I never—got over him." Her voice broke.

"I'm so sorry." Roslyn rested her hand on her friend's, and squeezed. "It sounds kind of like my situation." She went on to describe her own dilemma.

"Do you love him?" Toni questioned.

"Yes!" There was no question in her mind. "I do."

"Then stick with him. You'll be sorry otherwise," Toni advised.

But would she? After lunch, on the drive back, Roslyn wasn't so sure.

She was still undecided as she walked around her apartment an hour later. Breaking up with Ben would tear her apart. But how long could a girl wait for a commitment from the guy she loved? Who loved her too?

She loved Ben, with all her heart. But she also had self-respect. How long could she go on like this? She didn't want to be like her Aunt Ann. Neither did she want to force Ben into a marriage like her cousin. That would surely backfire.

She found herself praying for guidance.

Should she follow Sarah's lead and look for a guy who wanted a commitment? Or listen to Antonia and hold on longer for her true love to come around?

She plopped on her couch, burying her head in her hands. She was so confused! She felt like she was being split right down the middle.

And she owed Ben an answer tonight!

She swallowed, and, feeling thirsty, got up to get cold water from her refrigerator.

Standing by the fridge, her eyes lit on the "Save

the Date!" postcard from Sarah and Adam. It showed a photo of them, dressed up, in a park near their home. Sarah and Adam gazed lovingly into each other's eyes, clasping hands and smiling.

Gazing at their happy faces, pain pierced her like a knife. She wanted that. And she had to accept that it wouldn't happen with Ben.

She shut her eyes against the sudden onslaught of tears. No, she would never force him into an engagement. After he'd seen Sarah and Adam yesterday he'd been subdued, as had she. And she could imagine that it might spur him on to make a casual proposal.

But that's not what she wanted. She wanted someone who was 100% committed to her. Someone who wanted *her* in his life, forever.

She leaned against the fridge, the cold water bottle in her hand, and let out a sob.

It wasn't going to happen. And much as she loved Ben, she had to respect herself.

She had to break it off with him.

And she wouldn't do what Antonia had done. She would *not* just get married for the sake of being married to any guy.

She would live the rest of her life alone, single, if necessary. And try to make the best life for herself that she could.

***

Ben couldn't wait to get back to Roslyn's place.

He'd gone home, changed to a different shirt, sweater and jeans, and spent a little time on line since his brother had been unable to meet up with him. Finally, impatient, he headed back to her home twenty minutes too early. He just couldn't wait to see her. To declare his everlasting love, and propose to her.

The ring was in the fancy velvet box, inside a gold bag from the store, sitting beside him in the car. He glanced at it, unable to keep from smiling.

He pulled into her parking lot. Slipping the jeweler's box into his pants pocket, he left the bag and exited the car. He walked rapidly up the steps to Roslyn's front door. He rapped on it.

He heard movement, and after a moment, she called out. "Who's there?"

"Ben. I know I'm early," he said.

She opened the door, and he was shocked to see how pale she looked. Her eyes were puffy, and he knew immediately she'd been crying. He'd seen her like this on the day her grandfather had died. His gut clenched.

"What's wrong?" He went to pull her into his arms but she sidestepped.

"Come in. Sit down," she said, her voice wavering.

Something was wrong. He followed her inside and sat on the couch.

"Ben," she began. "I've done a lot of thinking."

Uh oh. That didn't sound like it was positive thinking.

"Yes?" he asked.

"And I—I think we should break up."

This time, his stomach dropped. "Roslyn—"

"Listen," she said hastily. "I gave you your chance. The eight nights of Hanukkah. But I would never force you to commit to me. You'd resent it eventually, and I want someone who will love me with no regrets. So, we need to split up."

He grabbed her hand. "I do love you, Roslyn."

"Not enough." She shook her head sadly. "And I love you too much to try to tie you down when you clearly don't want to."

"That's not true!" He stood suddenly. "Come with me."

She let him pull her to the table holding the menorah. "It's not sundown yet," he said, "but almost." He began lighting the candles with a hand that shook. He chanted the blessing, and after a few seconds she joined in.

When every candle was lit and the flames blazed, he turned to her and grasped her hand.

And dropped to one knee.

"Roslyn, I love you. I always have and always will." His words were solemn. He met her eyes, which were staring at him. He fumbled to remove the box from his pocket. "Will you marry me?"

She gave a soft gasp. "I—no, Ben."

"*No?*" He stared at her as shock reverberated through him.

She shook her head, withdrawing her hand. "Believe me, I know you're feeling forced to do this. After seeing my sister and her engagement ring yesterday you realized how badly I've been feeling. You didn't want to lose me. But that's not a good reason to get married—"

"I love you," he interrupted. "Your sister has nothing to do with it. You see, when I bought this ring, I wondered if you would say yes or no—and that's when it hit me. The uncertainty you'd been feeling all along. The doubt."

She shook her head again. "You just got the ring

because you thought I was going to break off with you if you didn't. You knew I felt bad that—that my sister got engaged after she knew her fiancé only a year. That I felt bad because she had a committed boyfriend and I—I didn't." Her voice shook.

"Wait a minute." He stood up, leaving the box on the table. "I can prove you wrong." And he would.

He dashed out her front door, without his coat. He fumbled for his keys and then ducked into the car. His hand closed on the bag handles.

Relocking the car, he sprinted through the frigid air back up to her condo. She was standing in the doorway, staring at him.

Shutting the door behind him, he turned to face her. "Look." He withdrew the receipt from the bag.

"What's this? The receipt?'

"Look at the date."

She studied it. "It's from Thursday."

"That's right." He grabbed her hand, and dropped to one knee again. "I decided *before* we saw your family that I wanted to marry you, Roslyn. I love you. I used to be afraid of marriage, but—with you by my side, I'm not. I want you. I want a life with you, I want it all. Total commitment."

Her eyes were filling with tears.

He opened the box, removed the shiny diamond, and held it out. "Will you marry me?"

"Oh, Ben—" she choked out. "*Yes*!" and she threw herself into his arms.

They tumbled to the floor in a tangle of arms and legs, and he kissed her furiously. "I love you. I love you."

"I love you, Ben," she whispered.

"I want to get married as soon as possible," he said as he kissed her all over. "I don't want to wait."

She laughed. "Me too!"

He pulled back to look at her. "We'll spend the rest of our lives together, loving each other," he said solemnly.

"Yes," she whispered. "You've won me over, Ben."

It had taken eight nights—but he'd won her heart.

And he would treasure it every day of his life.

EPILOGUE

First Night of Hanukkah
The Following Year

The menorah looked perfect.

Roslyn smiled as she placed the first candle and the shamash in their holders, ready for when Ben got home and they could light the candles together. Their first Hanukkah as husband and wife.

They'd had a beautiful wedding in October and honeymooned in Hawaii—like she'd always dreamed. Settling into married life had been easy and wonderful. They'd bought a house in between their two jobs and she'd been happier than she'd ever expected. Ben had been true to his word—he'd showed her how much he loved her every single day.

His key scraped the lock, and he entered the hall.

"Hi, sweetheart." He enfolded her in his arms.

She kissed him hard. "Hi."

It was already dark, and she had brisket and latkes waiting in the kitchen for their dinner.

"It smells delicious." He sniffed the air, grinning.

She smiled. "First we light the candles."

As they chanted the familiar prayer, Ben enveloped her in his arms, and she leaned into him.

Last Hanukkah had changed her life. Ben had shown her he really did want a lifetime commitment to her, and she'd never been so happy.

As if he read her thoughts, he murmured, "last Hanukkah I asked you for a chance to win your love again."

"And you did," she said, turning in his arms. She touched his face reverently. "I'm glad I gave you that chance."

As he bent to kiss her again, she knew the eight nights of Hanukkah would always be very special to them.

Hanukkah would always remind them not only of the miracle of the holiday—but of the miracle of their love.

Because he'd proven he did love her, and he'd won her heart and soul.

THE END

ABOUT THE AUTHOR

Roni Denholtz has published 16 romance novels and novellas. Her books have been nominated for the New Jersey Golden Leaf Award, Southern Magic Award and the National Reader's Choice Award. "Marquis in a Minute" won the New Jersey Golden Leaf Award for Best Regency Romance. She has also written dozens of short stories and articles for magazines such as "Baby Talk," "Child Life," "Modern Romance" and "For the Bride." She is the author of 9 children's books, published by January Productions. "Jenny Gets Glasses" was named #7 of the Top 20 Favorite Books of First Graders in a nationwide study by the Reading is Fundamental Group.

A former special education teacher, Roni also taught Writing for Fun and Profit for over 20 years in her local adult school. Many of her students went on to get published.

Roni is a member of New Jersey Romance Writers, where she served as president for the 2016 year; Romance Writers of America; and the Authors Guild. She served on the board of Noah's Ark Animal Shelter and was active in PTA, Marching Band Parents, and Robotic Parents when her children were young.

Roni and her husband own an independent real estate company, Jersey Success Realty, in northwest New Jersey. They have two grown, married children and a rescue dog.

Roni also enjoys cooking, photography, and travel. She is an avid reader and always has a book nearby.

Roni loves to hear from readers! Please visit her at www.ronidenholtz.com You can also find her on Facebook and Instagram.

ALSO BY RONI DENHOLTZ

Enchanted Vermont Nights
Return to Forever
Those Canyon Nights
Forecast for Love
Room for Love
One of These Nights
Stuck in the Saddle with You
Setting the Stage for Love
Borrowing the Bride
A Taste of Romance
Salsa with Me
Marquis in a Minute
Negotiating Love
Somebody to Love
Lights of Love